# Monster Mountain

# Thunderbelle's Spooky Night

For Christine Lo
K.W.

For James, with love,
G. P-R.

First published in 2007 by Orchard Books
First paperback publication in 2008

ORCHARD BOOKS
338 Euston Road, London NW1 3BH
Orchard Books Australia
Level 17/207 Kent St, Sydney, NSW 2000

ISBN 978 1 84362 617 6 (hardback)
ISBN 978 1 84362 625 1 (paperback)

1 3 5 7 9 10 8 6 4 2 (hardback)
1 3 5 7 9 10 8 6 4 2 (paperback)

Printed in China

Orchard Books is a division of Hachette Children's Books,
an Hachette Livre UK company.

www.orchardbooks.co.uk

# Monster Mountain

# Thunderbelle's Spooky Night

## Karen Wallace

Illustrated by

## Guy Parker-Rees

ORCHARD BOOKS

One night Thunderbelle woke up.
It was very dark. The wind made
a spooky noise in the trees.
Thunderbelle felt scared.

The next morning Roxorus zoomed by.
He waved, but Thunderbelle did not
wave back.

Roxorus ran into Thunderbelle's
kitchen. "What is wrong?" he said.

"I could not sleep last night,"
said Thunderbelle.
A fat tear rolled down her face.
"I am afraid of the dark!"

Roxorus rang the Brilliant Ideas
gong. **Bong! Bong! Bong!**
The other monsters came as fast
as they could.

Pipsquawk flapped onto her
favourite branch.
"Who has a brilliant idea?"
she squawked.

"We *need* a brilliant idea," cried
Roxorus. "Thunderbelle is afraid
of the dark."

Pipsquawk looked at Thunderbelle.
"Don't be sad!" she said. "Anyone can
be afraid of the dark."

Pipsquawk hung upside down on
her branch. "We will find a way to
make you feel better."

"How?" cried all the other monsters.

Pipsquawk swung back and forth and thought hard. She had her best ideas upside down.

"First we must wait until it is dark again," she said.

"Then what?" shouted the
other monsters.

"Then I will think of another idea!"
squawked Pipsquawk. She swung
upright again. "But while we are
waiting, we will have some fun!"

All the monsters thought this
was a brilliant plan. First they rode
on Roxorus's skateboard.

Then they played by the river.

Then they helped Mudmighty in
his vegetable garden.
Thunderbelle picked
some peas.

Clodbuster pulled up
a giant turnip.

And Roxorus
planted some carrots.

At last the sun
went down.

"Now what shall I do?" asked
Thunderbelle.
"Go to bed as usual," said
Pipsquawk.

"I do not understand," said Thunderbelle. "I am still afraid of the dark!"

"Wait and see," said Pipsquawk.

That night Thunderbelle woke up.
The wind made her curtains
flutter. She heard a strange noise.
It was very dark.
Thunderbelle sat up in bed and
burst into tears.

Pipsquawk flew in through
Thunderbelle's window.
"Come with me," she said.
"But I am afraid of the dark,"
cried Thunderbelle.

"Come with me and you
will not be afraid any more,"
said Pipsquawk.

Pipsquawk and Thunderbelle went
to see Clodbuster. He was staring
at the sky.
"Aren't you afraid of the
dark?" Thunderbelle asked.

"It is not dark," said Clodbuster.
"The moon is shining!"
Thunderbelle looked up. Clodbuster
was right. She began to feel better.

Then Pipsquawk and Thunderbelle went to see Roxorus. He was curled up in his cave. "Aren't you afraid of all the spooky noises at night?" asked Thunderbelle.

Roxorus shook his head. "They are not spooky," he said. "It is only the wind in the trees and owls calling. Listen!"

So Thunderbelle listened. Roxorus was right. The noises were not spooky at all.

"Let's go and see Mudmighty," whispered Pipsquawk. Mudmighty was lying in his hammock.

"Don't you get lonely at night?"
asked Thunderbelle.
"I am never lonely," Mudmighty said.
"There are millions of stars in the sky!
They look like shiny seeds!"

Pipsquawk took Thunderbelle
down to the river bank. The
water made a happy bubbly noise.
They looked up at the white
moon and the sparkly stars.

Thunderbelle heard the wind in the trees and the owls calling. Nothing felt spooky or lonely any more.

Something shone by the river bank.
Thunderbelle picked it up. It was
a smooth silver pebble.
"This is my very own star,"
said Thunderbelle.
Pipsquawk smiled. "Let's go home."

Thunderbelle put her silver pebble
under her pillow. She lay down and
closed her eyes.

"Good night," said Pipsquawk.
"See you in the morning."
But Thunderbelle did not reply.
She was already asleep.

# Monster Mountain

All priced at £8.99. Monster Mountain books are available from
all good bookshops, or can be ordered direct from the publisher:
Orchard Books, PO BOX 29, Douglas IM99 1BQ. Credit card orders
please telephone 01624 836000 or fax 01624 837033 or visit our website:
www.orchardbooks.co.uk or e-mail: bookshop@enterprise.net for details.

To order please quote title, author and ISBN and your full name and address.
Cheques and postal orders should be made payable to 'Bookpost plc.'
Postage and packing is FREE within the UK
(overseas customers should add £2.00 per book).

Prices and availability are subject to change.